Reviews for "Vincent the Very Vulgar"

5 out of 5 stars: **Loved this book!**
By: Amazon Customer

A charming tale with an important message to children about being polite. The book is beautifully illustrated and written in a way that kept my children engaged to the end. I look forward to more titles from this author.

5 out of 5 stars
By: Amazon Customer

Uniquely illustrated with a good story line, pretty much what you need from a child's book, loved it!!!

5 out of 5 stars: **I just would like to congratulate this author who I know personally!!**
By Amazon Customer

I just would like to congratulate this author who I know personally for producing this book, it is a great story and my youngest who is 8 commented on how he liked the pictures and the story too and he was even more impressed that he knows the author, looking forward to reading many more.

VINCENT AND RINGO VISIT TIDY WATERS
The second book in the "Vincent the Very Vulgar" series
Story by G Hake
Illustrations by J Sassi
Copyright © 2016 Gary Hake

For the memory of a person who always taught me to do the right thing, and for anyone who enjoys my work.

Special thanks once again to LB.

Other books by this author:
Vincent the Very Vulgar

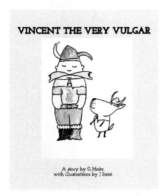

Follow Gary on:
twitter: @garyhakeauthor
facebook: @garyhakeauthor
web: www.garyhake.wixsite.com/garyhake

It was that time of year again...
Vincent wakes up and shouts to his dog,
**"Ringo, let's go on holiday! Pack as many
ragworm and banana skin sandwiches as
you can, we're going to stay at Tidy
Waters!"** Ringo excitedly begins to run around
gathering items for the journey.

Very early the next day, Vincent and Ringo are
ready to leave, **"All aboard!"** shouts Vincent, as
loud as he can, which wakes up everybody trying
to sleep.
With a boat full of food, off they set on holiday.

As Vincent and Ringo row their boat, they begin to get hungry. They stop for breakfast (which again is a ragworm and banana skin sandwich!) when they are greeted by a friendly group of birds and fish who ask them if they are lost and need help. Ringo begins to bark at the birds and fish and Vincent shouts at them also, **"No we are not lost! Go away and let us eat our breakfast in peace!"**
With that, they throw their crusts and left over banana skins into the water, which almost hit the fish!

After days of rowing, and rowing for days, they finally arrive at Tidy Waters, which is a beautiful, neat, clean and tidy beach with lots of people on holiday enjoying themselves. As they walk along the beach, Vincent shouts at people very rudely so he can put up his tent. **"Move out of the way!"** he shouts, as Ringo barks at them.

As they put their tent up, they stop for lunch and, once again, they drop their leftover sandwiches on the neat, clean and tidy beach.

After two days of sitting on the beach, and making a huge pile of rubbish, the other people on the beach begin to ask Vincent and Ringo if they will tidy up their mess. Vincent replies, very rudely, "Go away, you are spoiling our holiday, leave us alone!" Vincent and Ringo refuse to listen, and the pile grows bigger and bigger!

After three days, the other people on the beach decide to tidy up, so they put all of Vincent and Ringo's rubbish into their boat.

Later that day, Vincent wakes up and says to Ringo, "It's time to go home Ringo, let's go, and pack the tent away."
Ringo becomes upset and looks sad. Vincent sees this and says "We have to go Ringo, we've run out of sandwiches." Ringo packs the tent away as Vincent loads the boat.

As they leave Tidy Waters, Ringo notices that the boat is filling up with water, so he barks at Vincent. "What's the matter Ringo?" Vincent asks, and sees the rising water.
Vincent becomes angry as he notices the big pile of their rubbish that the people from the beach had put in their boat. "It's the rubbish Ringo, it's made our boat too heavy and now we're sinking!"

As the boat sinks, Vincent and Ringo find themselves in the water shouting for help! **"HELP US! HELP US WE'RE SINKING!"**

Some people in a nearby boat hear Vincent shouting and row over to help, but they can't get close enough to Vincent and Ringo, because of all the rubbish in the water.
"We can't get close enough to you" the rower says, "The rubbish is in the way."
Vincent then begins to shout at them, **"HELP US, OUR BOAT IS SINKING!"** But still the rower cannot get close enough.

Ringo begins to cry as he is too tired from swimming, and Vincent feels sad too, as he is also tired. Hearing all of the noise, the birds and fish return to help. "Are you ok?" the fish ask Vincent.

"**NO!**" shouts Vincent, "our boat has sunk and the rowing boat cannot help us as all of our rubbish is in the way, can you help us?"

The birds and fish replies, "But you were rude to us on your journey to Tidy Waters, and then you left all of your rubbish on the beach. Why should we help you?"
"Oh please help us, we promise never to leave our rubbish anywhere ever again. Please help us!"
"Do you promise to never leave your rubbish anywhere, and you promise to tidy up after yourselves?" ask the birds and fish.

"YES, YES!" shouts Vincent as Ringo nods, "Then we shall help you both ". The birds and fish say, as they began to eat the leftover bread crusts from the water, and pick up the banana skins and fly them away.

With the rubbish cleared and tidied, the boat finally rescues them both, and Vincent and Ringo say, "Thank you so much, we promise to clear our rubbish away and tidy up after ourselves, always".

From that day forward, and from this day back, Vincent and Ringo have **always** put their rubbish away neatly and tidied up their mess, everywhere they go.

THE END.

About the author...

Gary is an Engineering Teacher in Kent, United Kingdom. Inspired by both of his Son's love for reading he attempted in writing his own Children's book. His first book "Vincent the Very Vulgar" has welcomed some excellent reviews. Gary's previous occupations include being a toolmaker, Maintenance technician and an air conditioning Engineer.

About the illustrator...

Jen is a Head of Art and Photography at a secondary school in Kent, UK and enjoys sharing the knowledge of Art with the younger generation. Inspired by the magic found in children's books, Vincent has been created with a hint of nostalgia for all readers to enjoy his aquatic adventures.

Lightning Source UK Ltd.
Milton Keynes UK
UKOW07f0416041116
286807UK00001B/9/P

9 781367 216730